While You Are Sleeping

For Peewee

WHILE YOU ARE SLEEPING
A RED FOX BOOK 978 0 099 45697 1

First published in Great Britain by Hutchinson,
an imprint of Random House Children's Books

Hutchinson edition published 2006
Red Fox edition published 2007

1 3 5 7 9 10 8 6 4 2

Red Fox Books are published by Random House Children's Books,
61–63 Uxbridge Road, London W5 5SA
Addresses for companies within The Random House Group Limited
can be found at: www.randomhouse.co.uk/offices.htm

THE RANDOM HOUSE GROUP Limited Reg. No. 954009
www.**kidsatrandomhouse**.co.uk

A CIP catalogue record for this book is available from the British Library.

Printed in China

While You Are Sleeping

Alexis Deacon

RED FOX

We are the bedside toys.

Do you ever stop to think what we go through,
night after night, to look after you?

All day we sit as still as stone,

waiting, waiting, waiting,

but when the sun goes down
and we're absolutely *sure* you're sleeping . . .

. . . we get up.
We shake our heads.
We stretch our weary legs.
"Another long night
ahead," we say.

But what's this?
A new toy?

He'll have to help us with our work,
if he wants to join our crew.

Each night the whole room
must be checked.

Every cupboard.

Every corner.

We even peek behind the curtains,

and if we're feeling brave . . .

. . . underneath the bed.

But we can't stay long.
There's lots more work for us to do!

If you're too hot,

too cold,

or ill . . .

we try to make it better.

Bed bugs won't bite, we squish them flat.

We scare
bad dreams away.

And on that one night,
when you absolutely must not wake,
we make sure you don't.

We keep you safe no matter what.
That's our job, you see.

If you need us . . .

. . . we'll be there.

And when the sun comes up,
we use our last bit of strength
to crawl back to our places.

Just in time!

Why do we do it?
Why do we put ourselves through it,
night after night after night?
The new toy knows the answer . . .

. . . now he’s a bedside toy too.

Other critically acclaimed picture books by Alexis Deacon:

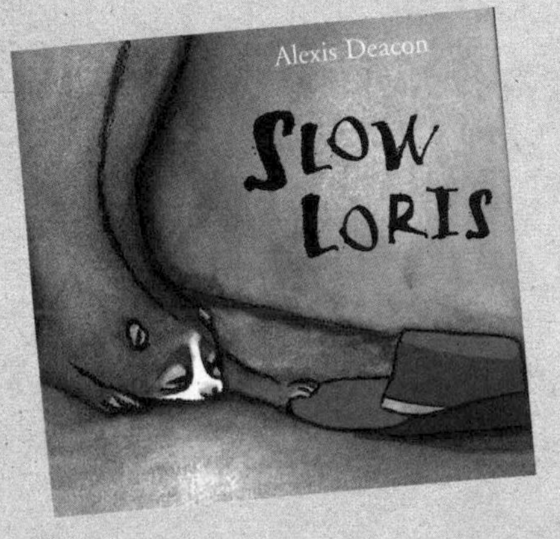

"Deacon's debut picture book displays admirable originality and draughtsmanship, and a great sense of humour" The Times

"One of those books that leaves you wanting more" Independent

"This is a really thrilling debut . . . Its originality jumps out of the covers" Guardian

"I loved the bold illustration and refreshing lack of sentimentality" Observer

"Alexis Deacon may well be Burningham's heir-apparent . . . Deacon's poignant and understated text is brilliantly served by his illustrations, which carry distant reminders of some of the best illustrators of the last 100 years and yet still remain uniquely his own" Sunday Telegraph

"Comic and touching . . . exquisitely expressive" Sunday Times

"Contains the sort of skill and imagination that most illustrators can only dream about" Sunday Times

"Cute and endearing without being at all cloying or sentimental, this book is another bull's-eye for Deacon" Times Educational Supplement

"Alexis Deacon is one of the finest of a younger generation of English illustrators for children . . . his horned monsters . . . seem distantly related to Maurice Sendak's wild things" The Economist